LIFE'S LITTLE FRUSTRATION BOOK

A Parody

By G. Gaynor McTigue

A Stonesong Press Book
St. Martin's Press   New York

LIFE'S LITTLE FRUSTRATION BOOK

Copyright © 1994 by The Stonesong Press, Inc. and G. Gaynor McTigue.

ISBN: 0-312-95215-5

Printed in the United States of America

St. Martin's Paperbacks edition/February 1994

St. Martin's Paperbacks are published by St. Martin's Press, 175 Fifth Avenue, New York, N.Y. 10010.

10 9 8 7 6 5 4 3 2 1

INTRODUCTION

Does life really stink? Perhaps not, but it's certainly fraught with enough irritants, foibles and annoyances to sometimes make us feel that way.

Take comfort. You're not alone in having to cope with daily aggravations. In *Life's Little Frustration Book* you'll find an abundant source of repressed vexations you can vent, share with others, grind your teeth over, have a laugh at. Things that, no matter how exalted our position in life, reduce us all to the hapless, vulnerable, sometimes bungling mortals we are.

❖ Introduction ❖

First and foremost, I will spare you the frustration of having
to read a lengthy, windbag introduction. Just permit me to express
a note of thanks to Sheree Bykofsky, Paul Fargis, Mitch Achiron,
Tracy Bernstein and my wife Beth. And, of course, to all of those
souls, witting and unwitting, without whom *(ahem)* this book would
not have been possible.

G. Gaynor McTigue

1 ❖ You're served a cup of coffee with a puddle in the saucer.

2 ❖ You pull a drawer out too far and dump the contents all over the floor.

3 ❖ You step on a wet floor with your socks on.

4 ❖ You have to try on a pair of sunglasses with that stupid little plastic thing in the middle of them . . .

5 ❖ . . . then check yourself out in a mirror the size of a credit card.

6 ❖ The person behind you in the supermarket runs his cart into the back of your ankle.

7 ❖ The hangers in your closet get all tangled up.

8 ❖ The elevator stops on every floor and nobody gets on.

9 ❖ The hot dogs come ten per package, the rolls eight.

10 ❖ Your dry cleaner puts staples in your $450 suit.

11 ❖ There's always a car riding your tail when you're slowing down to find an address.

12 ❖ You're put on hold and forced to listen to a three-minute rumba rendition of "Rhapsody in Blue."

13 ❖ You open a can of soup and the lid falls in.

14 ❖ Batteries are not included.

15 ❖ It's bad enough you step in dog poop, but you don't realize it till you walk across your living room rug.

16 ❖ You videotape a four-star movie using last week's *TV Guide*.

17 ❖ Your dentist has bad breath.

18 ❖ You put your drink down at a party and there are three more just like it when you go to pick it up.

19 ❖ The egg salad jettisons out the back of your sandwich when you take a bite.

20 ❖ The tiny red string on the Band-Aid wrapper never works for you.

21 ❖ The tip of your ballpoint pen leaves tiny blobs of ink on the page that smear on contact.

22 ❖ The little hanger loop on the collar of your coat breaks the first time you use it.

23 ❖ The library book you're reading has 23 pages of coffee stains right in the middle of it . . .

24 ❖ . . . and four pages of what you hope are chocolate smudges shortly thereafter.

25 ❖ The person sitting next to you in the theater hogs the armrest for the entire performance.

26 ❖ There's a dog in the neighborhood that barks at *everything*.

27 ❖ Your waiter removes your plate before you've finished that last tasty bite.

28 ❖ You can never put anything back in a box the way it came.

29 ❖ Department stores have scores of cash registers to take your money, but only one overcrowded cashier's window to issue refunds.

30 ❖ There are no hooks in the fitting room.

31 ❖ The germy metal tab on your beverage can dips into the soda when you open it.

32 ❖ A fire-engine-red sock accidentally finds its way into your load of white washables.

33 ❖ The waiter asks if everything is okay when your mouth is full.

34 ❖ Three hours and three meetings after lunch you look in the mirror and discover a piece of parsley stuck to your front tooth.

35 ❖ You open the wrong side of the milk carton.

36 ❖ The telemarketing rep not only interrupts your dinner, he mangles the pronunciation of your name.

37 ❖ You have to spread cold, hard peanut butter on a slice of soft bread.

38 ❖ The waitress refills your cup of decaf with regular coffee.

39 ❖ Your toasty shower turns into a scalding nightmare when someone flushes the toilet.

40 ❖ The child-proof medicine cap serves to remind you that you are still a child.

41 ❖ You pull on the toilet paper and the whole reel comes flying off into the toilet.

42 ❖ You drink from a soda can into which some-one has extinguished a cigarette.

43 ❖ You accidentally dial the same person you just talked to.

44 ❖ Your lobster salad sandwich turns out to be sea legs supreme.

45 ❖ It costs you $127 to frame a $6 poster.

46 ❖ You spend five minutes explaining your situation to someone on the phone who turns out to be the answering service.

47 ❖ You slice your tongue licking an envelope.

48 ❖ You open a magazine and a reply card comes fluttering out onto your lap.

49 ❖ Another one comes fluttering out several pages later.

50 ❖ Your tire gauge lets out half the air while you're trying to get a reading.

51 ❖ Someone sitting near you on the train passes gas every seven minutes for the duration of the trip.

52 ❖ People turn around and glare as if *you* did it.

53 ❖ You go out of your way to hold the door for someone and they walk right by without saying thank you.

54 ❖ You light a damp match and the flaring head fuses to your finger.

55 ❖ You're in the bathroom at a friend's house, the door doesn't lock, and their three-year-old kid is trying to push his way in.

56 ❖ You park at a curb and your car door scrapes along the sidewalk when you open it.

57 ❖ You write an address on an envelope, then realize it's upside-down.

58 ❖ You have to send it out anyway because it's your last envelope.

59 ❖ You're sitting in traffic on the freeway and a car comes whizzing by on the shoulder.

60 ❖ The edges of your potato chips are green.

61 ❖ People get annoyed when you ask them to remove their stuff from an available seat.

62 ❖ Two weeks after your permanent, your hair still smells like sulphured peaches.

63 ❖ Your refreshments at the movie theater cost more than dinner.

64 ❖ A station comes in brilliantly when you're standing near the radio, but buzzes, drifts and spits every time you move away.

65 ❖ The 20-minute wait estimated by the maitre d' turns out to be an hour and a half.

66 ❖ You call a business . . . are put on hold . . . wait about ten minutes . . . hear a click . . . then get a dial tone.

67 ❖ There are always one or two ice cubes that won't pop out of the tray.

68 ❖ You spill half the water in the tray trying to reinsert it into the freezer.

69 ❖ You have to pull your new lamp out of a box containing 15,000 foam peanuts.

70 ❖ No matter how tight you attach the hose to the outdoor faucet, it leaks, sprays and dribbles.

71 ❖ You have a popcorn fleck stuck to the back of your palette and your tongue can't reach it.

72 ❖ While in a restaurant bathroom, you see an employee emerge from a stall and walk past the sink out the door.

73 ❖ You see that same employee assembling your Salad Nicoise.

74 ❖ You bash your shin on the corner of a glass coffee table.

75 ❖ The car in front of you at the toll plaza doesn't realize it's an exact change lane.

76 ❖ There are no mirrors in the fitting room, so you have to model that scanty new bathing suit in front of the lunchtime shopping crowd.

77 ❖ You wash a garment with a tissue in the pocket and your entire laundry comes out covered with lint.

78 ❖ Garden gates always scrape on the ground when you open them.

79 ❖ They glue the inside paper liner to the cereal box, so when you go to roll it up you tear a big hole in it.

80 ❖ The drawstring of your sweatpants slips irretrievably into its sleeve.

81 ❖ You're running behind schedule with your dinner party and one of your guests shows up a half-hour *early*.

82 ❖ You forget to serve one of the dishes you made.

83 ❖ Your coffee cup is filled so high you can't put any milk or sugar in it.

84 ❖ Presumptuous salespeople call you by your first name.

85 ❖ You've got this one song in your head and it's driving you crazy.

86 ❖ There are three people on the sidewalk watching while you're trying to parallel park.

87 ❖ The children of your guests walk on your furniture with their shoes.

88 ❖ You fill out an application and put information in the wrong boxes.

89 ❖ The plastic wrap sticks to the roll and you haven't a clue where to begin peeling it.

90 ❖ You have to sit through 37 loud and obnoxious car dealer commercials during one evening of television.

91 ❖ You practically rip the skin off your fingers trying to open a beer bottle that isn't a twist-off.

92 ❖ You practically rip the skin off your fingers trying to open a beer bottle that *is* a twist-off.

93 ❖ Your doctor will charge you if you miss an appointment, but couldn't care less how long you wait in his office.

94 ❖ Your cassette player turns seven minutes of your favorite tape into spaghetti.

95 ❖ You can't find your ticket stub to get back in.

96 ❖ You staple a stack of papers but only one side of the staple goes through.

97 ❖ Your staple remover cannot handle this type of contingency.

98 ❖ You try to start your car while the engine is running.

99 ❖ You send money to a charity and a week later you get a letter saying thank you, but could you please contribute some more?

100 ❖ You wake up suddenly from a fascinating dream, and immediately forget what it was.

101 ❖ You fry your eggs on a pan you've forgotten to grease.

102 ❖ Four people in the middle of your row decide to leave during a pivotal scene in the movie.

103 ❖ One of them steps on your ingrown toenail.

104 ❖ You spend half of your Mexican vacation on the stool.

105 ❖ The rubber band breaks just before you get it around the package.

106 ❖ It scares the hell out of you.

107 ❖ The article featured on a magazine's cover is nearly impossible to find in the table of contents.

108 ❖ You get the wrong pictures back from the mail order developer.

109 ❖ Which means someone else has 12 shots of you sunbathing in the nude.

110 ❖ You finally find a pair of jeans that fit you to a tee, then discover they're button-fly.

111 ❖ You miss your exit and the next one is 17 miles away.

112 ❖ You get a shopping cart with one wheel that won't move.

113 ❖ You twirl your spaghetti and send a fine red spray across your chest.

114 ❖ Your favorite utility informs you that the repair person will arrive anywhere between 8 a.m. and 6 p.m.

115 ❖ You take an entire day off from work and the guy doesn't show.

116 ❖ Next month your rates go up.

117 ❖ The fitted sheet keeps popping off at the corner where your head is.

118 ❖ You have a 75% failure rate opening sardine cans with a key.

119 ❖ You accidentally spit in the face of the person you are talking to.

120 ❖ The person in front of you on the express check-out is 5 items over the limit (you counted) . . . and wants to pay by check.

121 ❖ The continuation of the newspaper article isn't on the page they said it would be.

122 ❖ You see the item you paid full price for at 60% off.

123 ❖ You take 36 photographs of the family wedding before you realize there's no film in the camera.

124 ❖ You step barefoot in melting tar on a hot summer day.

125 ❖ The chocolate coating on your ice cream pop slides off onto your hand.

126 ❖ You can't open the drawer because something inside it is sticking up, and you can't push it down till you open the drawer.

127 ❖ You have to cut tough steak with a plastic knife. On a paper plate. In your lap.

128 ❖ The person sitting next to you on the plane doesn't shut up the entire three hours.

129 ❖ You bite into a large piece of grizzle at a business lunch but are too embarrassed to remove it from your mouth.

130 ❖ You try swallowing it, choke, and have to cough it up in front of the entire restaurant.

131 ❖ You're standing in the midst of a very important group of people and get an intense itch in your crotch.

132 ❖ The clerk at the motor vehicle office treats you as if she were paying *your* salary.

133 ❖ You're asked for your telephone number and stupidly can't remember what it is.

134 ❖ You're standing at a bus stop and the driver pulls up 30 feet past you.

135 ❖ People start piling onto the elevator before you have a chance to get off.

136 ❖ You vehemently argue that you're in the right theater seat before it's pointed out you're in the wrong row.

137 ❖ The kid riding his bike down the wrong side of the street curses *you* for stepping in his path.

138 ❖ You forget to move your clock forward for daylight savings time and are in the shower when the matinee begins.

139 ❖ Your roll of Life Savers unravels in your pocket and gets all mixed up with your money and keys.

140 ❖ You have a two-minute coughing fit during a live chamber music recital.

141 ❖ Your glass in the diner has a lipstick print on it.

142 ❖ Your waiter wipes it off with his apron and puts it back on the table.

143 ❖ Another shopper in the supermarket asks you if you work there.

144 ❖ You forget to put the shower curtain *inside* the tub.

145 ❖ Your feet break through the sheets at the end of the bed into the cold morning air.

146 ❖ The guy in the next stall had *huevos rancheros* for lunch.

147 ❖ You get the hiccups just as you're being escorted into a job interview.

148 ❖ The announcement over the loudspeaker regarding your train sounds like the speaker has a sock in his mouth.

149 ❖ You sit on a wet seat but don't realize it till it's soaked through to your skin.

150 ❖ You pull all the mozzarella off your pizza with the first bite.

151 ❖ Your life has come down to watching hour-long shows advertising car polish and food dehydrators.

152 ❖ You misplace your glasses. Again.

153 ❖ You have to fly five hours wedged into the middle seat . . . in coach.

154 ❖ The person sitting in front of you puts his chair back all the way.

155 ❖ Seated next to you is a mother with a colicky baby.

156 ❖ You have to get up nine times to let her go to the lavatory.

157 ❖ You button your shirt with the first button in the second hole . . . the second button in the third hole . . . the third button in the fourth hole . . .

158 ❖ You sit down to a meal and dip your silk tie into the soup.

159 ❖ The long-awaited movie you taped cuts off ten minutes before the ending.

160 ❖ Your table is in the no-smoking section, but the one right next to it is in the smoking section.

161 ❖ The person before you didn't flush.

162 ❖ Breakfast at your hotel costs $16.75.

163 ❖ Later, you discover a place down the street with a $2.99 breakfast special.

164 ❖ Your French toast is crisp and golden on the outside, soft and runny on the inside.

165 ❖ You accidentally stab yourself in the hand with a lead pencil.

166 ❖ It leaves a little gray dot there for the rest of your life.

167 ❖ You're dying to eat that last hors d'oeuvre, but as a courtesy offer it to someone else first . . . *and they take it.*

168 ❖ Your Velcro doesn't Velcro anymore.

169 ❖ Your bookmark falls out somewhere between pages 250 and 400.

170 ❖ You arrive in town on a fine summer morning with your fly wide open and the white of your underwear showing through.

171 ❖ The mechanic charges you not according to what he knows, but what you don't.

172 ❖ Her name is Trish . . . she'll be your waitress . . . and she wants to know how you are this evening.

173 ❖ You spend countless minutes getting your hair just so, and the wind whips it into a dust mop in five seconds.

174 ❖ You dine at the trendiest restaurant in town and have to sit facing the wall.

175 ❖ You dial a number repeatedly and get a busy signal. When you finally get a ring, there's no answer.

176 ❖ You lean over to turn on the bathtub faucet and get doused by the shower.

177 ❖ You're one of the first to check in for a flight . . . and the last to get your luggage.

178 ❖ There's always one spoke on your umbrella that pops loose from the fabric.

179 ❖ You mail a card three days before Valentine's Day, and it gets there four days after.

180 ❖ You're on a long bank line, one teller is open, and two others are chatting behind the counter.

181 ❖ You press the trail mix button on the vending machine and out comes gummy bears.

182 ❖ The bill changer rejects your dollar seven times before accepting it.

183 ❖ Someone walks in on you while you're picking your nose.

184 ❖ People who came into the restaurant after you are served their lunch, eat and leave before you even get your appetizer.

185 ❖ The video you rented isn't rewound.

186 ❖ You wait 12 minutes at the bakery counter before realizing you have to take a number.

187 ❖ The red wine you pour during a romantic dinner dribbles down the side of the carafe onto the tablecloth.

188 ❖ You buy an album based on the one song you've heard, and all the other cuts are dogs.

189 ❖ Someone in the movie has a watch that beeps every half hour.

190 ❖ You have to come up with something to do every New Year's Eve.

191 ❖ You have to try on a pair of pants with a clunky anti-theft device dangling from one leg.

192 ❖ You bring a gourmet dessert to a dinner party and the host doesn't serve it.

193 ❖ You have to open and squeeze five little foil packets to get enough ketchup for one hamburger and French fries.

194 ❖ You're a large, and there are 13 extra-smalls on the rack.

195 ❖ You have to open gifts in front of a large group of people.

196 ❖ You reach under the table to pick something off the floor and smash your head on the way up.

197 ❖ You pour orange juice on your cereal.

198 ❖ You flush the toilet at a party and to your horror it rises . . . and rises . . . and rises . . .

199 ❖ Waiting to use the bathroom is that attractive person you've been trying to impress.

200 ❖ You forget to put the top on the blender and let 'er rip.

201 ❖ You can never split the English muffins evenly.

202 ❖ Your movie seat lists to starboard.

203 ❖ You just got your car washed and a bird decorates the hood.

204 ❖ The series of road signs you've been following suddenly stops in the middle of nowhere.

205 ❖ There's something underneath the paper you are writing on that makes your pen go all crooked.

206 ❖ The person in front of you on line is holding a place for five other people.

207 ❖ You have to remove 14 pins from your new shirt and aren't sure you got them all.

208 ❖ You plop down into a chair later on and discover the one you missed.

209 ❖ You had that pen in your hand only a second ago—a *second* ago—and now you can't find it.

210 ❖ You're walking in a fast-moving crowd and your shoelace comes untied.

211 ❖ You have to shop in an overheated department store in your winter coat.

212 ❖ Leaving a building, the people in front of you stop in the doorway to chat, blocking your exit.

213 ❖ You tune in to a game to get the score and the announcers blather on endlessly about everything but.

214 ❖ You get your penis caught in your zipper.

215 ❖ People get their fingerprints all over your photographs.

216 ❖ You're seated at a dinner party between two incredibly boring people.

217 ❖ You're seated at a dinner party between two interesting people, but they talk only to the person on the other side of them.

218 ❖ Someone has an extra ticket to a meaningless game between two awful teams and you have to sound ecstatic and come up with a good excuse at the same time.

219 ❖ You take someone special to an expensive restaurant and the waiter has to ask, "Who gets the veal?"

220 ❖ You immediately forget the name of the person you've just been introduced to.

221 ❖ You're in the middle of a blowout argument with your spouse and the doorbell rings with your first guests.

222 ❖ Your mouth is filled with clamps, cotton wads and suction devices, you're told not to swallow, and your dentist is called to the phone.

223 ❖ You have to inform five different sales people in the same store that you're just browsing.

224 ❖ You take a gulp of cold coffee from a cup that's been lying around too long.

225 ❖ It's easier to get an audience with the Pope than talk to your doctor on the phone.

226 ❖ Rather than admit his ignorance, the salesperson gives you wrong answers to your questions.

227 ❖ You never know if someone has received your thank you note.

228 ❖ Somebody stirred their coffee with the sugar spoon and put it back in the bowl.

229 ❖ You're late for an important appointment and a friend you haven't heard from in years calls you up.

230 ❖ You arrive at the toll booth just as they're changing shifts and counting receipts.

231 ❖ Your toe is being strangled by a hole in your sock.

232 ❖ You buy a product in a blister package and can't, for the life of you, separate the plastic from the cardboard.

233 ❖ The long-awaited green light lasts only ten seconds . . . and the car in front of you stalls.

234 ❖ You have to thread a little metal ball into a little metal slot to hang up your pants in a dark hotel closet.

235 ❖ You don't know if the Lee you're writing a business letter to is a man or a woman.

236 ❖ Traffic always seems to move more slowly when there's a traffic cop involved.

237 ❖ The supermarket bagger puts your boxed layer cake in sideways and the entire top of the icing sticks to the cellophane window.

238 ❖ You have to order drinks at a noisy bar three-deep with people.

239 ❖ The aerosol can is still one-third full when it runs out of propellant.

240 ❖ Someone in the locker room asks to borrow your comb.

241 ❖ You can never fold a road map back the way it was.

242 ❖ You can't look up the correct spelling of a word in the dictionary because you don't know how to spell it.

243 ❖ They show people getting needles on TV.

244 ❖ People behind you on a supermarket line dash ahead of you to a counter just opening up.

245 ❖ You have to throw away an otherwise good appliance because it would cost more to fix it than buy a new one.

246 ❖ A car waiting to pull out of a driveway has its nose sticking into the lane you're driving in.

247 ❖ Your glasses slide off your ears when you perspire.

248 ❖ There's a swarm of gnats buzzing your head—and your head only—at an outdoor cocktail party.

249 ❖ You have to repeat three times to the deli clerk what goes on your sandwich.

250 ❖ Still, he gives you mayo when you asked for mustard.

251 ❖ The lady sitting next to you has enough perfume on to knock you out.

252 ❖ You're dressed in your lightest hot-weather clothes and the restaurant is freezing.

253 ❖ Just before you enter a room full of people, you discover a nasty run in your stocking.

254 ❖ In the book you have to read, illustrations don't count as pages.

255 ❖ Your telephone cord shrivels up into kinks and knots.

256 ❖ The subtitles in the foreign movie are white-on-white.

257 ❖ Your paintbrush leaves long black bristles in its wake.

258 ❖ You go to kiss someone on the cheek, but they move their head the same way you do, then you both move back in the other direction, and finally your faces crash somewhere in between.

259 ❖ Your voice suddenly breaks into falsetto.

260 ❖ The local news feels obligated to show footage of every boring parade that marches through your town.

261 ❖ A guest with a cold gives you a big wet kiss hello.

262 ❖ On the mouth.

263 ❖ People who borrow books from you don't return them.

264 ❖ Your seat on the airplane is next to a bank of lavatories.

265 ❖ Your stuff keeps falling out while you're trying to push it into the overhead.

266 ❖ The whole plane is watching.

267 ❖ The menu at the diner has 475 items to choose from.

268 ❖ The waitress asks you after 30 seconds if you're ready to order.

269 ❖ You're watching a dubbed movie and the lip-synching is out of whack.

270 ❖ The bus boy has obviously never heard of deodorant.

271 ❖ He refills your water glass every time you take a sip.

272 ❖ You walk briskly into a turnstile that doesn't turn.

273 ❖ You have to use a public phone whose mouthpiece is grimy, smelly, and gross.

274 ❖ You botch the opening of your guest's expensive bottle of wine and have to push the cork in.

275 ❖ The music you used to rock to is now Muzak.

276 ❖ The pushbutton faucet in the public bathroom blasts water all over you.

277 ❖ You have to stand at the "Please Wait To Be Seated" sign several self-conscious minutes before someone comes over to help you.

278 ❖ You break your sterling silver serving spoon digging out a scoop of ice cream.

279 ❖ You split your pants at the beginning of the workday.

280 ❖ You address, stamp, and seal an envelope, then realize you've left something out.

281 ❖ You can't shake a static-charged piece of paper from your hand.

282 ❖ You bite into a sandwich in which the plastic has not been peeled from the bologna.

283 ❖ It's easy to reach the lawyer on the phone . . . until you pay him a $3000 retainer.

284 ❖ You rub on hand cream and can't turn the bathroom doorknob to get out.

285 ❖ The radio station doesn't tell you who sang what.

286 ❖ You have to collate 35 curled-up sheets of fax paper.

287 ❖ You're dozing in a chair . . . your leg falls asleep . . . and the doorbell rings.

288 ❖ The gas station makes you pay for your gas before you know how much you need.

289 ❖ You set the alarm on your digital clock for 7 *p.m.* instead of 7 *a.m.*

290 ❖ You agree to a free trial issue of a magazine, then can't stop it from coming.

291 ❖ You're sitting in the airplane with your earphones on upside down.

292 ❖ Friends with young kids call you up before eight on Sunday mornings.

293 ❖ You can't get the window shades to roll up evenly.

294 ❖ Associates feel compelled to snicker "half a day?" when you leave work on time.

295 ❖ A jet passes overhead just as you're getting important info on the radio.

296 ❖ The computer you bought last year is a dinosaur this year.

297 ❖ Your felt-tip pen dries up in mid-sentence.

298 ❖ The phone in the government office you're trying to call is busy eight hours a day, five days a week.

299 ❖ The bank pays you 3% interest so they can lend your money to people you wouldn't dare to.

300 ❖ You're pedaling your bike hard up a steep hill . . . and the gear slips.

301 ❖ Someone got to all the black jelly beans before you.

302 ❖ You're thrilled to get front row seats to a major play, and the actors spit all over you.

303 ❖ The "state-of-the-art" ski equipment you bought five years ago is now considered unsafe.

304 ❖ Three-hundred-sixty-two other golfers decided to take the day off, too.

305 ❖ You get wet sand in your bathing suit.

306 ❖ You bite avidly into what you thought was a seedless grape.

307 ❖ You pull a chair up to a desk and . . .
whack! . . . your knees don't clear.

308 ❖ Your zipper jams halfway.

309 ❖ Your serving of fish has five bones per
bite.

310 ❖ You cut off the little plastic thing that attaches the price tag to the garment, but can't find the other end.

311 ❖ The item you purchased from a mail-order catalog is about half the size you thought it would be.

312 ❖ Your Sunday afternoon is filled with the sound of lawn mowers, power drills and chain saws.

313 ❖ About half the pages in the magazine have no numbers.

314 ❖ The top of the ketchup bottle is encrusted with remnants from meals past.

315 ❖ You tell someone you haven't seen in a long time how good they look, but they don't return the compliment.

316 ❖ You've got a two-prong extension cord and a three-prong plug.

317 ❖ You climb into your warm, cozy bed . . . turn out the light . . . get all relaxed and comfy . . . then realize you forgot to do something.

318 ❖ You start a fire with the flue closed.

319 ❖ People let their kids run, play and shout in the library.

320 ❖ You make a horrible mess trying to dispose of dead flowers.

321 ❖ A house guest bad-mouths the town you live in.

322 ❖ The person on the other end of a business call is eating while talking.

323 ❖ The office calls you up while you're on vacation.

324 ❖ The water either dribbles out of the water fountain . . . or splashes you in the face.

325 ❖ The plastic anchor you put in the wall turns when the screw does.

326 ❖ You accidentally flick on a stereo with the volume turned all the way up.

327 ❖ You can't get the plastic bag around the edge of the garbage can.

328 ❖ They cut your hair way too short, and there isn't a damn thing you can do about it.

329 ❖ The tiny cinder you brush off your clothes leaves a black streak in its wake.

330 ❖ A piece of foil candy wrapper makes electrical contact with your filling.

331 ❖ You have to dig through a messy garbage can for something you threw out by mistake.

332 ❖ The car behind you blasts its horn because you let a pedestrian finish crossing.

333 ❖ Key information on a product's label is blocked by the price sticker.

334 ❖ Your stack of file folders slides off your desk.

335 ❖ You wake up one morning and hate all your clothes.

336 ❖ You clip your toenails and have no idea where they landed.

337 ❖ The most interesting TV program listed is on a channel you don't get.

338 ❖ Your hamburger falls through the barbecue grill.

339 ❖ A mangy stray cat rubs up against your leg.

340 ❖ You take a picture of your thumb.

341 ❖ You get four pennies back with your change.

342 ❖ The key breaks off in the lock.

343 ❖ You stink at miniature golf.

344 ❖ They don't take credit cards.

345 ❖ You can't get the plastic cover of the battery compartment back on.

346 ❖ You pay for your dry cleaning and walk out without the clothes.

347 ❖ Your rice comes out crunchy.

348 ❖ You're duped into opening five envelopes a week that look like checks.

349 ❖ Someone put the ladle for the blue cheese dressing in the French.

350 ❖ The juice from a package of chicken leaks all over your groceries.

351 ❖ Something falls under the bed and you just . . . can't . . . reach it.

352 ❖ Your drug store is well stocked with candy, soda, and beach balls . . . but is always in short supply of the health aids you need.

353 ❖ You strike two computer keys at the same time.

354 ❖ You tell an off-color joke and nobody laughs.

355 ❖ Your neighbors don't argue. They scream.

356 ❖ Your organic bran muffin crumbles into a thousand pieces when you try to butter it.

357 ❖ You press "Stairway to Heaven" on the jukebox and it plays Bing Crosby's "Happy Birthday."

358 ❖ You're enjoying a quiet morning at home when a pair of Jehovah's Witnesses show up at the door.

359 ❖ You take a shower and forget to wash your hair.

360 ❖ You leave the milk out.

361 ❖ The nail scissors work great on one hand, lousy on the other.

❖ G. Gaynor McTigue ❖

362 ❖ You have to endure the awkward, amateurish small talk between your local newscasters.

363 ❖ Your blind date shows food when chewing.

364 ❖ Something is preventing the refrigerator door from closing and you can't figure out what it is.